This Book Belongs to:

Made in the USA
Coppell, TX
08 December 2023

25638547R00063